Bits and Pieces

Short Stories
from a Writer's Soul

Barking Spiders Publishing 2011

ISBN# 978-0-9839320-4-8

Fiction

Copyright 2011 C J Heck

All rights reserved
First Printing - 2011

Request for Information should be addressed to:

CJ Heck
705 W. Long Avenue
Du Bois, PA 15801
814.249.1777
cjheck@barkingspiderspoetry.com

Other books by CJ Heck:
Barking Spiders (and Other Such Stuff)
Barking Spiders 2
Me Too! Preschool Poetry

Cover Design: CJ Heck
Copyright 2000

Printed in USA 2011
Barking Spiders Publishing

Du Bois, PA

Dedicated to W. Joseph Parrish
and in loving memory of Joanne E. Parrish

With all my love,
respect, and admiration.
I love you both

Cath'

Introduction:

Tour of a Writer/Poet

Go in through the eyes of a writer
deep into her alphabet mind.
Ideas like flotsam and jetsam
dodge poetry fragments and lines.
Beware the dark shadows of memory,
knife-sharp and bloodied by time,
or gentle, orgasmic and sensual,
swirling eddies, some without rhyme.
Softly notice the spirit in hiding.
Tiptoe past the bruised heart mending there,
knitting poems, pearls strung on a necklace,
her unfinished jewels everywhere.
Take note on your tour of this writer,
the outside, no different, you see,
but inside, my God, a passion abyss,
the writer, the woman, the me.

CJ Heck

CONTENTS

Bits and Pieces

Short Stories
from a Writer's Soul

by CJ Heck

Barking Spiders Publishing
Du Bois PA

Old People in The Park

Old People in the Park

One afternoon last fall, I grabbed a sweater and a book and, after stopping at Dunkin' Donuts for my favorite coffee to-go, I headed to our town's park. A people-watcher by nature, I love walking the paths through the park and then studying different people from my reading bench who also love going there.

Not too far into the park, I picked out a bench under a colorful birch where I could read for awhile. Just across from me, an elderly man was talking with his grandson who was seated on the bench next to him. The boy was six, maybe seven years old, with the most incredible blond curls framing what someday in his maturity would be a very handsome face. He had huge eyes that looked adoringly up at his grandpa, as though searching his face for answers to his many questions and they were holding hands.

When looking at any beautiful child, I can't help but think of something my mother used to say, "With all of the beautiful children in the world, I wonder where all the homely adults come from." I smiled, partly because she had been right, but also because I missed her terribly and the memory brought her closer to me.

I overheard the boy ask his grandfather, "Grampa, why are there so many old people in the park every day?"

The old man was quiet, thoughtful, for a minute. Then I heard him clear his throat. He let go of the boy's hand and slowly stretched an arm around the youngster's shoulders, pulling him closer.

Then in unhurried words, he told the boy, "Well, son, I suppose they're just too alone at home to want to stay there. See, sometimes, old people need to be with other old people. Here in the park, they can share their favorite jokes and maybe play a lazy game of bocce ball or play some checkers, just to pass a little bit of time together."

Then, looking down at the pigeons gathering on the ground around the bench, the old man reached into the pocket of his tan jacket and pulled out a small brown paper bag. He handed it to his grandson. The boy thanked him thoughtfully, reached into the rumpled brown bag, and with a great big smile, began tossing pieces of popcorn, one by one, to the pigeons, favoring a gray one with a pronounced limp.

As he did this, he asked the old man, "Grampa, why do they all call out names and wave at everybody that comes to the park?"

The grandfather cocked his head to the side, thinking, and as though measuring each word, he slowly said, "Hmmm, I guess it's just a way of keeping their minds alive and well-oiled. You know, by remembering a person and their name. After all, your mind is just like a muscle and all muscles need to be exercised. Remembering everyone's name and face is like a private game they all play, and maybe it even helps them to ignore their pains and problems for awhile."

The boy nodded his understanding and continued to feed the pigeons, taking his temporary job quite seriously. Then, spotting a gray squirrel that had darted out from under the bench to steal a kernel of popcorn, he jumped up and stomped his small sneaker on the sidewalk and said a loud "Shoo!"

The squirrel scampered off, but, of course, this also frightened the pigeons who instantly took to the air and it was so cute that it made me smile. Then the boy sat back down beside the old man, obviously disappointed by the sudden turn in events.

The boy sat quietly for awhile, as he watched the old people in the park. As I mentioned, I'm a people watcher and I followed where his eyes traveled. They stopped first on a couple of elderly men playing a game of checkers on a stone table. Then they moved on over to settle on a group of three even older men having what seemed to be a heated verbal exchange.

As he looked from one little group to the other, he asked his grandfather whether he thought the men playing checkers ever got tired of doing that. "Do they just sit there every day doing the same thing for hours and hours?" Then without waiting for an answer, he glanced at the men who seemed to be arguing, and asked, "What do you suppose they're so upset about, Grampa?"

The old man smiled lovingly at the boy. He cleared his throat and, in a slow, determined voice, he explained to his grandson that for some of the old folks, the daily checkers games were a way of making some sense out of a changing world that they didn't feel a part of any more. He said, in a way, it was like keeping them in touch with a world they *did* know -- and it also got them out of their recliner chairs and away from their TV sets for a little while, too.

The old man stared into space quietly for a moment. Then he went on to explain that the three men who seemed to be in a heated discussion weren't really arguing. They antagonized and criticized each other a little bit, but just to keep their juices flowing, not to be mean or hurtful. He said sometimes they even acted a little bit wise by bragging, or maybe griping, about the good old days. You know, talking about their old girlfriends or teasing the others about their old girlfriends. The boy giggled at his grampa's explanation and then in typical little-boy fashion, he wiped his nose on his sleeve.

By now, the pigeons had again begun to congregate at the boy's feet, tentatively at first, but then with a little more fervor. It always amazed me how the feed-ees recognized so easily which feet belonged to the specific feed-er, because somehow they always knew and went straight to them.

The boy stuck his hand once again into the rumpled brown bag and brought out his next offering for the hungry rascals on the ground below. Both of them sat in silence, watching and grinning as the greedy winged goblins jockeyed into position for the next morsel dispensed from the small hand.

The boy then turned his face up to look into his grandfather's eyes and he asked him how long everyone stayed here in the park and how they knew when it was time to go home. The old man sighed. His eyes were still focused on the pigeons. At first, I thought he hadn't heard the boy, but then I saw him lovingly pat the blond curls on the top of the child's head. The grandfather told him they mostly stayed till it started to get dark, or sometimes, until it just got too cold to be there any longer. Then, one by one, they waved goodbye, again calling each other by name just as they did every day when they first got there. Then they went home again and, for many of them, back into the past again, too.

The boy nodded, then he smiled up at the old man again, and both renewed their feeding ritual of the pigeons. After a little while, the boy asked his grampa how he got so smart and knew so much. The old man told him that when you got to be his age ... well, there were some things you ... you just... *knew*.

With that, the youngster looked up at his grandfather with a concerned look on his face and said, "I love you, Grampa, and you're NOT old. You're like a shiny red apple. You're ripe and ...you're *j u s t right*."

The old man laughed out loud and, God help me, I did, too. Maybe it was the dwindling light, or it might have been a trick of my eyes, but I could swear I saw the lines in his face smooth right out. He looked a full ten years younger and I was surprised to find a tear on my cheek as I watched the old man swipe at his eyes when his laughter had finally subsided.

Slowly, the old man looked up into the sky. He told his grandson they should be getting along home now. As they rose to leave, the grandfather replaced the empty rumpled brown paper bag in his pocket and stood up to leave. One by one, the others in the park raised an arm and called him by name, almost in unison.

"Bye, Gabe."

He, in turn, did the same. "Bye Herb, Sam, Max, Shorty, Charlie, Gib. Later, fellas."

"Hey, Gabe. We still on for checkers tomorrow at nine?" Called one man sitting next to the men who were playing checkers at the stone table.

"Sure, Sam. Lookin' forward to it," was Gabe's response.

Overhearing the exchange, I was sure God would forgive his little white lie ...

And, the last I saw of the little boy who was at the beginning of his life, and the wise and loving old man nearing the end of his, they were walking slowly back down the path through the park, hand in hand.

A Box for Good Will

A Box for Goodwill

As a friend, Martha had come to help yet one more time, and she watched as Gayle set the empty cardboard box on the floor, as she had done so many times before. The box was labeled for Goodwill, carefully penned in black permanent marker with large block letters nearly fifty years ago.

From deep in the closet of her room, Gayle began by pulling out an old blue suit. It had faded over the years, but Martha could see in Gayle's eyes that the memories still had not.

Softly, Gayle smoothed the sleeves that dangled flat and empty. Then she stroked the trousers hanging over the smooth wooden hanger. Gently, Gayle brushed the dust from the collar and lapel, and then Martha heard a quiet sigh. Just as she had feared, Gayle's resolve had melted away once more.

Gayle's face was pale as she turned and faced Martha, who silently patted a spot beside her on the bed. Gayle sat down, and again they talked and remembered.

Gayle spoke of long ago, how the sleeves had encircled her in warm, secure hugs. The trousers had covered lean muscular legs; legs that were slightly bowed; legs that loved to dance.

Then Gayle told Martha again about what she missed the most -- the heart that beat just below the lapel of the old blue suit; the heart that beat with love for her.

For over fifty years, the suit had stood sentinel, loyally guarding both Gayle and her memories. Now Martha watched as Gayle carefully replaced the suit and closed the closet door.

Then, through quiet tears, Gayle asked once more, "How could all of that ever fit in a box for Goodwill ..."

The Unopened Letter

Unopened Letter

The letter came on Monday, over a week ago. Maggie had been absently wading through the morning's harvest of mail, as she usually did during her lunch hour. Predictably, it reaped the usual bills, flyers, and grocery store ads, when she suddenly spotted the familiar masculine scrawl. Maggie was stunned.

After all the years of checking the mail, there it was, a pearl among the cow pies. She marveled at how the letter felt as she turned it over and over in her hands and then wiped at a tear that was threatening a slow getaway down her cheek.

After nearly an hour, Maggie still didn't know whether to open the letter or not, so she dropped it on the cherry table in the foyer. It sat there for nearly a week, mutely resting between the potted ivy and car keys, marking time, patiently waiting for her decision.

It remained unopened, of course, but Maggie was pretty sure what it said. She just couldn't make herself open it and read the words -- she knew they were angry -- that was a given. She also knew the words were probably written to demand in yet one more way, her whole future and one more chance -- and quite frankly, she loved her autonomy and was flat out of any more chances.

Maggie tried so many times to tell Jonathan he needed help. Abuse was abuse. It didn't matter whether it was emotional, physical, psychological, sexual or verbal -- God knows, he had been proficient in all of them -- it had hurt and it had been unnecessary.

She loved him, true, but she loved herself and valued her safety even more -- and now this letter. Well, it's too late, she argued. By moving away, she was finally free and that's the way it's going to stay, she thought -- and now this damned letter! Then again, what if he wrote to tell me he got help and therapy?

Maggie walked through the foyer a thousand times and each time, she stared at the letter. She even picked it up and held it close to her heart once -- as if her heart could tell by sheer divination that the words didn't say what she knew they did. She thought, maybe if don't read it, the words will somehow change and say what I need to hear, but then, Jonathan was never into apologies or admissions of wrongdoing -- forgiveness either, for that matter. "Damn it to hell and back! What a sorrowful waste of a stamp!" Maggie shouted into the empty foyer, creating an eerie echo.

For a solid week, even Maggie's nights were plagued by the letter -- open it, don't open it, open it, don't open it. By the following Wednesday, Maggie had had enough. She marched angrily into the foyer and grabbed the offensive letter. First she folded it in half, then quartered it, and finally, she stuffed it roughly into the back pocket of her blue jeans.

Ha! There! Now it would be safe from misbehaving hands and, with it out of sight, her mind wouldn't be tempted to breach its unspoken ceremonial rule to grant her permission to either touch it or want to open it.

Within a few hours, Maggie found herself in a quandary. She was unable to ignore the letter or throw it away. She wasn't sure how long she walked around with it in her back pocket. She only knew it began to burn her heart, then blister her mind, until finally, it even scorched her self-control.

It wasn't until she saw her jeans, letter and all, in the washer, twisting and turning in the soapy water, that she was even aware of what she'd done. When she saw them in the washer, she suddenly realized she had been cleansing and purging the past. It was just as well ... maybe now, she would find some peace at last

Stoker's Gift

Stoker's Gift

Stoker had never felt so alone. He was freezing and he missed Mama. It was dark where he was, and it was bouncing up and down so bad that it was hard for him to sit still. There were huge tears in his big brown eyes and tears were even overflowing his eyes and making trails down both cheeks, just like before.

It was cold in this place and he was glad he had his winter coat. The tear trails were freezing up and that made his face feel funny when he moved.

He didn't like this place and he wanted to go home. He wanted Mama, but all he could do was sit here and remember -- but remembering was sad. Remembering hurt ...

(Yesterday)

The snowstorm had begun right after dinner. It was the most frightening thing Stoker had ever been through. He had been afraid, so afraid in fact, that his fear was like a *real thing* that he could almost reach out and touch.

The wind had been terrible and loud and long. It didn't even snow like any snow he had ever seen before. This snow had come at him sideways and, when it touched him, it was like a thousand embers burning him with fire.

He was thankful Mama was there. She coaxed him down into the place where they hid from the storm. She held him tightly, and enveloped in her hug the way he was, he almost felt safe. When he remembered the warm and safe feel of her love, new tears slid down his cheeks.

During the long, scary night, the awful storm showed no signs of letting up. Even the friendly moon had hidden from the wind and snow. Usually Stoker could see it peeking at him between the branches of the trees high above their home.

The wind blew wildly. It had made such a terrible sound, like a whole lot of someones screaming and moaning.

Stoker sat huddled with Mama that long night down under what used to be their home. Now there was nothing left of home. Home had buckled under the weight of the heavy snow. Here and there, he heard parts of it being thrown all around them by the angry wind.

Above them, he remembered seeing one big part of home that had fallen. Now it was leaning and teetering back and forth precariously. Another part of home crashed against something, and right below that was where they sat huddled together in its shelter.

Each new time he thought about how frightened he was, more tears sneaked out of his eyes, following all of the others on their trip all the way down to his chin.

"Mama, I'm so scared! Hold me tighter!" Stoker cried. "When will it end?"

"I know, Stoker, I know. I'm frightened, too." His mother had answered with the wind carrying her words off in other directions. He had to listen closely to hear the rest of what she said. "I don't know when it will stop, son. We'll be all right if we just stay together. Don't move from here, no matter what happens, little Stoker. Promise me."

Although Stoker had no way of knowing why she would ask him for his promise, he agreed. "Okay, Mama. I'll stay right here, I promise."

All through the night, the wind raged and the snow came at them sideways. Mama tucked Stoker tightly to her, wrapping her arms snugly around him to keep him safe and warm.

Whenever he cried out, she did her best to comfort him. "Hush now, little Stoker, try to sleep. Mama's here, and I love you, little man."

Just before dawn, there had been an enormous crash. Stoker suddenly felt a heavy weight come down on him -- it had been so heavy he could hardly breathe. He called out to his mother,

"Mama! Mama, where are you?" But all Stoker could hear in return was the screaming of the wind.

"Mama, what was that loud noise?" Again, the only answer he heard was from the wind and the pounding of his own heart.

Stoker wanted to run, but he remembered his promise to Mama. He would not move from this spot, no matter what happened. He wanted to scream and yell and run as fast as the wind all around him, but Stoker kept his promise. He didn't try to get out from under this heavy thing.

Stoker sat quietly, listening for Mama. He sat waiting with fear in every part of his body making him wish he could run, but he stayed right where she made him promise to stay. Mama would be proud.

Stoker didn't know how long he waited -- maybe he even fell asleep for awhile. He only knew that he couldn't feel the sideways snow anymore and he was warm.

All of a sudden, he was aware of voices. They were loud and he could hear them above the wind which had now died down to only whistle. The voices frightened him and he remembered calling out to his mother again. "Mama! Mama! Please, Mama, I'm here! I'm here where you told me to stay, no matter what happened! Please, Mama! I'm scared!"

Stoker waited, listening for her answer. When it didn't come, he started all over again, calling and pleading.

"Over here, Johnny! Here! It's coming from under this fallen tree! Help me get this cable attached and we'll pull the tree off."

"You got it, Mike!"

Stoker continued to call for his mother. He could hear a lot of sounds coming from above. Some were the sounds of someone moving around, someone's feet crunching in the snow. Some sounds were mechanical sounds, like big machines, and that made him call out even louder. Stoker was terrified, but he kept his promise to Mama. He stayed there.

"Okay, Johnny. Now, pull!" The winch screeched into gear and the heavy wire cable noisily began to do its job.

Slowly, the huge weight was lifted from Stoker. His eyes were shut tight and he was too frightened to open them. Still, he called for Mama.

"What have you got there, Mike?" Johnny called. "Can you see what's making the racket?"

"Aw, Johnny, get over here! You've got to see this. " Mike answered, above Stoker's cries for his mother. "C'mere, and hurry!"

Johnny ran to where Mike stood looking down into the hollowed out area. Mike glanced over at Johnny. "Well, I'll be ... never saw anything like it. We'd better call Frank up at the Ranger Station. You have a cell phone in the truck, don't you?"

Johnny said he had one right there in his pocket and he handed it over. He dialed the number for the Park Ranger. Like Mike, his eyes never left the newly hollowed out area where the tree had rested only minutes before.

Stoker continued to call for his mother. Where was she? Why didn't she answer him? He was still too afraid to open his eyes.

With a series of electronic beeps, Johnny got through on the cell phone. "Hey Frank. John here. Well, sir ... what we've got here is the dangedest thing. We have a mother bear and her cub. No, sir, the mother bear is dead -- crushed by a huge tree which we removed. No sir. Cub's okay. She shielded the cub. He was safely tucked in under her. Frank, she still has her arms, er ... her paws wrapped around him, and him bawling out such sad sounds! Geez, Frank. It's like she *knew*."

There was a pause, then Johnny continued. "Yeah, uh huh. Can you get the Animal Control people out here right away -- maybe make some arrangements for a new home for the little guy? Yeah, I agree. Thanks, Frank." With that, Johnny pushed the button and ended the call.

"Johnny? What'd Frank say?" Mike asked, since he could only hear Johnny's side of the conversation.

Johnny quickly wiped at his eyes with his shirt sleeve. "He's going to make some calls, Mike. In the meantime, he'll get a truck up here with a cage to transport him. This little guy will be sad for a while, but he'll be okay.

Ya know, John, Frank said what you and I have been only thinking ... this little bear cub received the *ultimate* gift of a mother's love."

Christmas at Mel's

Christmas at Mel's

A broken neon sign flashed "Mel's" atop a small darkened bar on the edge of town. The air was heavy with stale smoke and beer, blending faintly with the odor of dried spit on unclean bodies.

Sadie sat at a small table alone pondering the world and its problems, two drinks past actually seeing beyond the unkempt nails on the chipped Formica in front of her. The lines in her face were knit as if by a palsied hand dropping stitches here and there where a pox scar decided to roost.

For Sadie, this was home -- at least until tonight's john, Mr. Empty Glass and Full Libido, swaggered up and invited her to the nearest no-tell motel. Life sucks, but it was her life. Feeling in control, a spider in her web, she threw back another drink and waited.

The hours passed and Sadie now slumped in the chair at her favorite table at Mel's. With each drink, the world's problems faded further, until she was only mildly conscious that she had more than enough of her own.

Merry Christmas. Yeah, yeah, so what? she asked indignantly.

Sadie slowly counted the empty glasses lined up in front of her on the table. Seven. Nice. Rhymes with heaven. How 'bout that. She studied the half empty glass that was still in her hand with the same intensity a demented gypsy might, upon watching her favorite crystal ball suddenly deflate before her eyes.

Tired, the lines in her face met in an intricate pattern just above her penciled brows as she pondered her situation through the booze fog. Damn Mel. Damn his twinkle lights. Damn things hurt my eyes. Fuckin' barkeep, he had to put twinkle lights in here ... as if anyone wants to see the graffiti better, she cackled to herself.

Sadie watched as the room with its new holiday lights blinked, first red, then green, then yellow through the gently swirling smoke. She threw back the rest of her drink. It made her want to puke, that's what it did.

Who the hell cares if it's Christmas Eve? Every day's the same to me, she thought. I'm just a workin' woman tryin' to make a buck.

Bad enough, everywhere you go, bells are ringin' on corners, music blastin' outta radios, snow and slush in every step you take, and all that fancy decoratin' to remind you, you're fuckin' alone. Merry Christmas ... yeah, Merry Christ-my-ass! Cash registers are ringin' big time, too, Sadie thought, with a bitter smile.

Damn. Business was slow this time of year. Every john she knew was probably home playing Santy Claus with the kiddies and Husband Of The Year with the wife. What a joke, she thought.

What they really want, I give 'em. What they really need, I give 'em. They're all the same. It's a fuckin' joke, she thought ... only the joke's on me. I'm the one who's sittin' in a blinkin-stinkin' hellhole all by myself.

Sadie set empty glass number eight at the end of the line on the table and raised a finger at the barkeep for another drink.

Just then, a shadow fell through the swirling smoke to settle eerily on Sadie's table. It was strangely blinking in mixed colors through the empty glasses in front of her. Surprised, she looked up to see one of her regulars standing there. Finally, she thought to herself, and 'bout time, too. Already a plan had formed in her mind to do him fast and then get some shut-eye. She gave the john her best crimson smile.

The man leaned down and handed Sadie a folded bill. With a sad smile he said, "Go home, Sadie. This one's on me, and ... and well, M-Merry Christmas to you."

Then he turned and walked back through the swirled and blinking smoke to the door and back out to the street with Sadie staring slack-jawed at the door closing slowly behind him.

Damn, if that don't beat all, Sadie thought, as she unfolded the fifty-dollar bill. Then she scooted her chair back, pushed herself away from the table, and for the first time in years, Sadie's face softened into a genuine smile.

The Hound Dog and The Crone

The Hound Dog and The Crone

Our town put a wonderful walking path down by the river a few years ago, complete with benches, porta-potties, flower gardens, totems carved by a local artisan, a wooden bridge, and all sorts of wildlife. It's a rare day that you don't see ducks, groundhogs, heron, deer, and even an occasional skunk along the scenic three-mile walkway.

Last Saturday, I was reading on one of the benches. Even with my eyes closed, I would have known it was fall, because the rich scent of decaying leaves hung sweetly in the air.

I watched as some Canadian geese flew overhead and then had to laugh at a honking straggler trying desperately to catch up and take his place in the perfect "V". It really was a beautiful day, a really fine day.

I was minding my own business and enjoying a rare day off from my writing and editing, when I saw the strangest thing. The more I thought about it, the more I wanted to share it ...

This all came about as I was turning a page in my book. I looked up for only a second and, on a bench sort of kitty-cornered across the path from me, I noticed a heavy-set old woman noisily gumming a soda straw which was poking out of the hole in a Pepsi can. Watching her, I almost laughed because she reminded me of a hungry baby nursing at the breast of its mother.

The woman's corpulent face was even older than ancient. Her many wrinkles had wilted into tiers, like icing spread on a cake that was still too warm yet for icing. Her eyes were deeply set and nearly hidden, like two dark asterisks set in among the folds of flesh.

I tried not to stare. I tried to turn away.   Failing miserably at both, I tried even harder not to laugh, I really did, and I didn't actually lose that battle until I saw her dog and what he considered his role to be with this strange woman.

At first, I only noticed the woman, but all at once, with a high-speed upward-outward motion, a hulking canine face popped out from in between the woman's legs down at ground level. I thought, my God, that is the ugliest dog I have ever seen!

The dog's face was framed on either side and above by the woman's long pink skirt and it's face was nearly engulfed by its own myriad of wrinkles of the hugest kind. His eyes were like two lumps of coal stuffed deeply into a large wad of brown dough. The mouth, a gaping slobbery hole, housed a pink tongue that hung down, almost touching the bully-boy collar around its neck.

Just above the mouth, also poked way into the brown dough, was what I presumed to be its nose.

The total picture was one of insane hilarity -- the stout head above, and the massive ugly twin below, peering out from between the woman's legs. Ironically, the wrinkled and toothless woman perfectly mirrored the droll and homely animal beneath her.

That's still not when I lost my battle to laughter. Up to this point, I managed to contain myself pretty well.

The old woman finally finished her Pepsi and rose from her bench. She slowly shuffled toward a trash can bolted to a fence post by the edge of the sidewalk.

The dog waddled along just behind her. After dropping the soda can into the barrel, she turned her head to the side and with a series of revolting sounds, belched loudly and hawked up a wad of phlegm -- a loogie of vast proportions -- which she promptly spat onto the sidewalk. Without missing a beat, the dog waddled over to the mess and promptly "cleaned it up" for her.

I was so busy trying to keep my gag and retch reflexes in check that I missed where the two went after that, but when I recovered, I took a quick peek. The old woman was back on the bench, the dog below, its enormous head again neatly framed in the pink folds of cloth and once more peering out at the world from between her legs.

It was that final picture and the improbable role reversal between dog and human that finally eroded my self-control and I drowned in a sea of my own laughter.

My only thought was, thank God I didn't know her ... and I grabbed my book and ran before I peed myself.

Valentine for an Old Love

Valentine for an Old Love

Katie blew the dust off of an old size six shoebox that was tied with an ivory ribbon. Years ago, she had carefully tucked the shoebox in a camel-back steamer trunk in the attic. There, it had rested for years -- until today, the same as every Valentine's Day, for the last thirty years.

Inside was one of her most cherished possessions: a valentine that was never sent. The love it represented flourished a long time ago, nearly a lifetime now, Katie thought. Funny, it was still as fresh in her mind today as the scent of the roses he brought her every Wednesday, just because a Wednesday was the day that they first met.

A deep sigh escaped her as she allowed herself this time to remember. They had been so very much in love, but so many miles and years were now between them.

The youthful he and she had long since moved on, each taking a different path through life, but so many times Katie felt regret for what might have been, had she been free. It was just like the words of a song she had once heard. God knows, it *is* sad to belong to someone else when the right one comes along. The pain of loss was still fresh in her heart and she knew it always would be.

Katie traced the embossed flowers on the card with her finger. I'll always love you, she thought. I'll always care -- love like that only happens once -- but I'm eternally grateful that I did know it. You're forever here in my heart and one more time I wonder what might have been, had I put a stamp on this card and dropped it into the box.

One more Valentine's Day had come. As she had on so many before this, Katie allowed herself to remember. I can still see your head making its familiar dimple in the pillow where you are. I wonder, can you sense my thoughts in your dreams while I lay inept at sleep? Do you ever reach out to me with your own thoughts? Would you hear me if I whispered, I want you, I need you, I love you, through my mind?

Katie brushed away a tear. Then she kissed the valentine and sent out the familiar wish from her heart to his: "For what we had, I wish you love."

Then, replacing the valentine in its size six cardboard home, she retied the ivory ribbon and tucked it carefully back into the steamer trunk to rest for another year ...

Just Passing Through

Just Passing Through

People who know me, know I'm well-grounded, practical, fairly logical, painfully honest, and I don't believe in love at first sight. Heck, I even wrote a poem about that once, but that's for another time. I do, however, believe in *something* at first sight -- but wait, I'll tell you what happened. You decide for yourself.

It's always been curious to me, what a single memory can call up from the recesses of your mind. A certain smell, a taste, even a sound you heard long ago can be recalled, almost relived, just as clearly as if it happened only minutes ago.

I remember a day like that, and it lingers softly in my memory. I can still feel, and even taste, the gritty dust blowing hot across my face on that sweltering summer's day. I can still hear the ding-ding-ding at the old-fashioned red and white gas pumps, as someone filled their gas tank -- and I can still smell the mingled aromas of diesel and gas.

As I recall, it was late August, during what we called the 'dog days of summer'. I was on a road trip to nowhere in particular, just going from here to there and taking a few days in which to do it.

Cars, back then, didn't have air conditioning, and I
remember it was stinking hot that day.
I had stopped for gas and a cold drink at a gas
station somewhere in Oklahoma, along a two-lane
road. I remember the hot wind blowing dust all
around, and it covered everything with a gritty light
brown powder.

Not quite ready to get back inside the steamy car, I
sat on a large rock under the only tree I saw within
miles, savoring the ice cold soda and wiping the
sweat and grime from my face and neck with a wet
paper towel from the ladies room.

Absently, I looked up and there was a man, a perfect
stranger, getting out of a dented and rusty old blue
pickup parked at the side of the road. Funny, I even
remember that his truck had a huge yellow peace
sign painted on the side.

Well, the man was walking straight towards me, and
even now, I'm not sure why I was so mesmerized by
the sight of him, but I was. When I close my eyes, I
can still picture him, striding towards me in run-down
brown leather boots, and the wind was pleasantly
ruffling up his sandy-blond hair.

When he got closer, I could see a roadmap of lines in
his tanned face and he was squinting at me through
the most extraordinary ice-blue eyes I had ever seen,
then or now, years later.

When he caught me staring, he casually touched a
finger to his hat, which was rakishly cocked to one
side, and threw me a wink, a quick nod, and a
crooked smile. "Ma'am."

That was all he said, but it was enough -- I had heard the sexy drawl. To this day I only hope my mouth was closed ...

He was muscular and tall, and his long legs moved him along in a slow, bowlegged stride -- a stride that literally reinvented the swaggered strut. His walk was as pure as poetry. I'm almost embarrassed to admit it, but as he passed by, my eyes were drawn to the back of the tight, worn blue jeans and the perfect male butt that filled them.

It wasn't that he was Marlboro Man handsome, because he wasn't, not really. What he did have was a sexy rugged look, a masculine sensuality that hinted of riding sweaty horses, squinting into the sun all day and sleeping out under the wide bowl of stars at night. It was all of that, and him so perfectly packaged in those tight worn jeans and blue plaid shirt with little pearl snaps and rolled up sleeves. All of it together, just like that, somehow whispered seduction.

I'll be honest, my emotions ran high that summer afternoon. Maybe it was my love of westerns as a child that it hit me like that, I don't know -- and yet the only thing that ever passed between us was a look, a wink, a nod, and that crooked smile. But I'll never forget that day when I fell -- not in love -- but definitely *something*, by the side of the road in the middle of nowhere, with a perfect stranger, a man I never met, someone just passing through.

Yardsticks

Yardsticks

The early autumn day was still warm enough to make her sweat. Kathryn smiled as she remembered her late mother's words to her when she was a young girl.

"Remember always, Kathryn, ladies don't sweat. Ladies perspire."

The salty breeze wafting over the water felt good as it gently teased the corners of the tablecloth up and out, like checkered wings. It also mercifully cooled the, *ahem*, perspiration that had glued the wisps of hair to her forehead.

From somewhere nearby, cicadas in love were calling out to each other in the trees. Their haunting melody mixed curiously with the waves, the soft clinking of silverware, and the distant laughter of children playing in the dwindling daylight on the beach below.

Kathryn was celebrating her last full day of vacation with a hot fudge sundae. Both were few and far between, and both had been fully savored, the vacation, day by lazy day, and the sundae, bite by delectable bite.

The best hot fudge sundae she had ever eaten had been in San Francisco, down near the water at the Chocolate Manufactory in Ghirradelli Square. That had been back in the early seventies, now nearly a lifetime ago, she thought, with a sigh.

Through the ensuing years, every time she had allowed herself this treat, a comparison took place in her mind. Each hot fudge sundae she ordered from some new place was measured against the invisible Ghirradelli Square yardstick.

Of course, those were minimal indulgences, because she wanted to maintain her figure, but the time between them built up such a delightful anticipation, making the stretches between indulgences much easier to handle.

Funny, until that very moment, Kathryn hadn't realized how many of those invisible yardsticks she actually carried around with her these days.

She had just turned fifty-nine. Admittedly, she had arrived at that age both kicking and screaming -- after all, no one ever *consciously* decides to be middle aged. Ultimately, however, thoughts of the *alternative* to getting older washed over her and, with a feeling of resignation, she bathed in all of the positives of actually being *allowed* to live that long.

Good grief! Kathryn had another sudden epiphany. She realized that she even studied other women around her who were her age, or near it, with yet another invisible yardstick in hand.

While never model-beautiful, she supposed she could have been considered a striking woman. She still had her figure. She worked hard to keep it, too, although admittedly, gravity was beginning to coax some parts of her slightly lower.

Her hair had recently begun to silver more at the temples and other grays were salted in liberally now, too, as if in afterthought. She smiled, deciding at last that the total effect *could* be considered attractive. Besides, she felt she had honestly earned the grays -- after all, she was a grandmother several times over.

Kathryn still noticed, and secretly welcomed, when a masculine head turned in her direction for a second look, every now and then. She couldn't know, and would have denied it had she been told, but their attraction to her came from a certain feminine enigma that surrounded her in public -- she appeared to be mysterious.

There was a gentle, child-like naiveté in her facial expression, which contradicted the sensual, at times almost haughty, self-assurance she exuded in both her walk and her manner. However, if you were to ask Kathryn, she would probably tell you she was merely being aloof.

Men thought, now here was a woman who drew your attention. She could walk into a room and own the room. Here was a confident woman who looked comfortable in her clothes -- and a woman they enjoyed imagining even more comfortable *out* of them -- thus, the enigma. But Kathryn wasn't aware of those things. What she did know was, the masculine heads that turned her way were divinely better than looking in a mirror -- and much more flattering, too.

She sat back in her chair, not wanting this last day to end. The sea breeze still felt wonderful. Maybe she would sit here just a little while longer. The sun was making its descent into the distant trees and she was suddenly struck by the silence. When had that happened? The lilting laughter of the children, even the drone of the cicadas, had disappeared sometime during her reverie about her various yardsticks.

The comparisons of hot fudge sundaes or other women her age was one thing, but Kathryn felt guilty, at times, when her mind eased on over to compare the men she had known in her life. She knew she shouldn't compare -- each deserved to be thought of as separate, an unique individual, but she rationalized that everyone did it and she couldn't help doing it either.

It wasn't that she even had a huge number of men to compare -- she didn't actually -- but the ones who had been in her life, had been there for a darn good reason. She eventually came to see that each of them played a specific role in who she now was.

Each had unknowingly brought with him a valuable lesson, or lessons, that she was to learn. After all, aren't we all products of our environment? Everything that happens to us changes us, making us who we were destined to become.

No, she decided, she would save her yardsticks to think about at another time. God knows, there were many nights just before sleep would allow her entrance, when her comparisons and mindless contemplation of life would be much better spent ...

With that decided, Kathryn stood and adjusted her skirt. Then, lifting her chin for maximum effect, she walked proudly and confidently to her car.

The Return

The Return

Gillian grabbed her bag from the luggage carrousel as it noisily passed in front of her. Finally. It had been well over an hour since her flight landed. The airport had grown, and changed, since she was last here, but then, so had most other airports since 9/11.

Pulling the handle up, she tilted the suitcase onto its wheels, and pulled it behind her through the terminal to the automatic doors and the sidewalk. There, she found a taxi to take her back to face the memories . It had been more years than she wanted to think about, since Gillian had been in the Keys. She had made a fateful decision here twenty years ago, one that changed her life forever.

Until now, she had been unable to gather the courage to face the Keys again, or the mystical time she had spent here. With a sigh, she had to admit to herself -- nor had she found the courage to face him again, either.

Not so, the memories. Unbidden and haunting, she carried them with her always, treasured and fiercely guarded. She realized with a deep and growing resignation, now she would hold onto them forever, because it's all she would ever have.

The decision she had made so long ago turned out to be the wrong one -- it had only taken her a few hours to see that, but sadly, by then it was already too late.

Coming here today was no mistake. She knew it would be devastating, and the hardest thing she would ever have to face. Now it truly was too late.

Gillian was popped out of her reverie when the cab driver stopped the cab at a corner directly across from the beach. She had forgotten how really beautiful it was here.

There was so much about the Keys she had missed and she was surprised and yet glad that the weathered building still stood; however, the once brightly painted facade was now only a faded patchwork of condemned signs and crumbling plaster.

Its boarded windows were long past feeling the warmth of the sun. She felt such a clash of emotions, finally standing here after all these years and remembering. Only by steeling her heart with a deep breath, was she able to climb the steps to the spacious and once vibrant veranda.

She looked around for a place to prop her suitcase and noticed that the front door was literally hanging off its hinges. Why anyone could just open the door and step inside ... again steeling her nerves and gathering as much resolve ad she could muster, Gillian forced the entrance door aside.

The once magnificent foyer brought another flood of memories and her breath caught in her throat in a sob, surprising Gillian. She could almost hear the soft music coming from the ballroom to the right, where they had danced until three in the morning.

The stairs that flowed up from either side of the foyer were higher than she remembered, and also very rickety. Ignoring the obvious safety hazard, she began to climb and now realized that the trip up was almost as difficult as the trip back in time.

In ruins thick with dust, and thicker still with memories, she felt her past and present collide. Gillian sat down hard on the top step and allowed her tears their freedom. The pain and sorrow flowed for what might have been, and she watched as each cleansing tear dropped on the aged and dirty floorboards.

It had been right to return. Here, in this place, she could allow herself to remember and grieve and the healing could finally begin. Gillian's memories enveloped her, one right after another ...

Barefoot and holding hands, with all of their dreams so new, they walked down these same steps and then across the street to the water's edge. She remembered looking down at their clasped hands. She couldn't tell where her fingers stopped and Michael's began and how wonderful that felt.

With their pants rolled up mid-calf, they had flirted with the waves and he wrote her name in the sand with his big toe and they had laughed until they cried.

She recalled how the vivid colors of the sunset had blended the blue-green water right into the sky as they packed up their things and put on sandy shoes to leave the beach.

We were so happy, Gillian thought, as a fresh wave of pain gripped her heart. We talked about him, and me, and we whispered of us. And after making love, we would lay basking in the afterglow with my head resting in the cradle of his shoulder. Her heart ached as she thought about that last night together. She realized that she had never felt such joy and sweet abandon before, or since.

They never spoke of anything that might get in the way or, if something did, how they would push it aside -- they never gave a thought to an end at all. They even assumed her abusive marriage was over. After all, she had left Theo for Michael. She had called and told him so.

Dear Michael, who was kind and good, an honest man who knew instinctively how to treat her, always with love and respect -- abuse wasn't even a word that Michael knew.

A gentle caring lover, Michael had known how to both give, and receive love. What they had was tender and beautiful and oh, she had loved him!

Then out of the blue, it happened. Theo played his trump card. Weeks after she had left him, he arrived unannounced on Michael's front porch when they returned from the Keys.

He reminded her they were married and he wanted her back. Of course, he had appealed directly to her highly-developed sense of right and wrong -- he had been a master at pouring on guilt for even the smallest infraction. In his words, Gillian had been adulterous and Theo would be magnanimous. He would forgive her. He promised things would be different and he told her she owed him another chance. Against everything that her heart was screaming, she had made her decision.

With a sigh, Gillian realized it had been right to return here to the Keys -- even if it was twenty years too late. It was time for her to face the past. How she wished she had called and told Michael she made a mistake, but there are some things that once done, can never be undone.

Michael had begged her to stay. He warned her that Theo would never change. She had hurt Michael beyond words -- she had hurt them both -- and there wasn't a day that went by that she didn't regret her decision.

Getting through Michael's funeral today would be the most difficult and painful experience of her life.

Some days are diamonds, some days are dust, and some days ... well, some days can never, ever, be anything but both .

Michael, I will never go barefoot again without thinking of you.

The Cottage by Salty Brook

The Cottage by Salty Brook

The dusty lane was very narrow. Little snippets of grass peeked through here and there between the deep ruts where I walked. I didn't really care where the lane was going. I had decided I would just follow wherever it took me. So, we continued along together, snaking through lofty fragrant pines to eventually follow along beside a little brook that gurgled and sang such lovely songs.

Lost in my thoughts, the dewy morning was only a memory by the time I noticed how the sun now warmed my shoulders from high above the trees.

As I rounded a small turn, the lane suddenly widened into a clearing. There I saw a small wooden hand-lettered sign tacked to a post just above a black metal mailbox which read: The Cottage by Salty Brook.

A little further down, the lane stopped altogether, dead-ending in front of a small cottage nestled in among even more stately pines.

The cabin looked tired, like a trusted old friend basking in the sun of his golden years. It had certainly seen better days, however, it also had an unmistakable "cared for" look. The weathered boards were now a faded grey and the curtains at the windows were yellowed and worn. On the wide front porch, two small boys sat playing and I slowed my walk to return their friendly waves.

The yard was square and wide, spreading all the way to the woods on either side and then around and behind the little house. The grass was sparse, but what was there was well taken care of.

There were toys strewn about the yard, and two red bicycles were parked as if patiently waiting for their young riders to return.

I almost missed the little girl as my eyes first swept the yard. She was sitting under a gnarled and ancient apple tree, with a homemade rag doll in her lap, humming softly to herself. A fragile child, she had the biggest blue eyes and her delicate face was framed in beautiful golden ringlets. She looked to be about five.

When she spotted me standing there, she put down her doll and ran over to me. At first she seemed shy, peeking up at me with those big blue eyes, and toeing the ground with a sandaled shoe. Then suddenly, she spoke in a rapid succession of questions and statements, which were all strung together, as one long one.

She asked, how did I get there, where I was going, and where have I been. Then she told me all about her family and finally, she asked me what my name was. I couldn't help but laugh. This adorable little waif had immediately stolen my heart with her gentle innocence.

I don't know how long we sat there talking in the shade of that gnarly apple tree sitting cross-legged, indian-style, on the grass. After a while, I simply noticed that our large and small shadows had gradually lengthened at our sides.

One by one, I answered all of her questions. I told her my name and, in turn, she shared hers and the names of six siblings. She told me they didn't go to the school in town. Their mama taught them at home. Then she told me all about their trips into town, again stringing all of her words together like the pearls on a necklace.

"The other kids in town all laugh and point at us. They say we're shabby and poor, but mama says it's okay. She says we should treat others the same as we would like them to treat us, and she says those kids just don't know any better, so we shouldn't blame them.

When I asked Papa if we were poor, he said no, we weren't poor. He told me we're very rich in the things that really matter. We just don't have a whole lot of money."

Her mom and dad then came to the patched screen door on the porch. "It's time for supper," her mother called.

With a wave to me, my little friend got up and ran toward the front steps. One by one the others all came, and as each of them stepped through the doorway, they gave their mama a kiss in passing.

The mother called out and asked if I would join them

for supper, "There's always room for more." When I entered the clean and tidy cabin, I saw that she had already set a place for me at the long wooden table.

The moon was peeking through the clouds and all of the shadows by the gurgling brook were gone when I finally left the Cottage by Salty Brook. There was a new coolness to the pine-scented air, but I wrapped their love around me like a cloak and wore it home.

Half Past Five

Half Past Five

There's a sewer drain in town on Peck's Corner. At
half past five each evening, the street lamp flickers
on, near where gentlemen routinely take a leak after
leaving the nearby Raven's Wing Pub.

The ritual is something they've been doing for years,
and no one even seems to notice, except for the
smell of piss when you step outside to the sidewalk. it's
bad, but only the vermin care and, believe me, there
are plenty of vermin near the sewer drain in town on
Peck's Corner. That's where it happened ...

Oh? You haven't heard? Well, I saw a body there as
I walked by the corner to the Wing. This was half past
five on Monday. The chimes from the clock in the
courthouse tower told me it was so, and when I
called, that's what I told the authorities.

He was sitting near the drain where the smell was
awful. His head was in his lap, resting between the
legs which were all askew and bent at impossible
angles.

The arms hung down, elbows bent and facing
out, with the hands resting on top of the head --the
head that was in his lap -- just above the flaming red
hair.

The hands were posed in the flaming red hair with the middle fingers broken and pointing at the sky

He was sitting in a pool of his own blood, his mouth frozen in a scream that no one will ever hear, but the eyes, the eyes ... I will never forget the eyes. The vermin had eaten both eyes.

Will anyone ever know the horror they saw on Peck's Corner near the Raven's Wing Pub, just before half past five ...

Mr. Beggar Man

Mr. Beggar Man

Mr. Beggar Man, you were such a gentle soul. Every day, you were dressed the same in a stained red plaid shirt, a brown felt hat speckled with bird poop, and saggy-baggy pants that stopped just above two heelless shoes that were see-through to feet with no socks.

So many mornings I walked by your corner, putting money in your cup, if only to borrow one of your smiles when I had none left of my own. I always knew that the one you gave would be the one that found those I had only misplaced for a while.

Countless times we shared a lunch, as you did with so many others. Sometimes hot soup from the deli across the street and, other times, half of my tuna sandwich from home.

You, in return, shared your wooden pallet to sit on, but never once a conversation. All the while, you never missed a beat as you continued to pass out your glorious smile to everyone who glanced your way as they hurried by.

I've often wondered what happened in your life to make you take up residence on that corner, only to die cold and alone. I'm saddened to know the smiles you apportioned to others were your only living legacy.

I know you are missed by many, even the many shopkeepers who so often shooed you away. I hope you knew what your smile meant to me ... and I regret never knowing your real name.

Waiting For a Greyhound

Waiting For a Greyhound

In the early morning hours of a Baltimore Monday, I
saw you this morning. You were just another nameless
lady sitting by yourself on a dirty bench in the
Greyhound Bus Station.

You wore a long red coat, a hat and a large brown
suitcase rested on the floor between your knees. Like
me, you were obviously waiting for an early morning
ride. Unlike me, your hat was pulled down tightly to
hide a swelling monument of love --sorry, I couldn't
help but see.

The matching handbag, you gripped two-fisted,
leaving only the sleeves of your red coat to wipe the
sadness from your eyes. My God, how could so much
misery share a dingy bench?

Red-coat lady, what happened to collapse your
world? Who, or what, was it that made you feel
so sad?

What could have happened to make your whole life
fit inside that suitcase, and why was that the only
thing between your legs at two a.m.?

I figure it had to be a man, and not a very nice
one, so no one would blame you for leaving. Maybe

wasting minutes felt better there in a bus station, crying softly, waiting for a ride, with your suitcase between your legs, instead of him.

It's merely speculation on my part, but I suppose yesterday's hopes and tomorrow's dreams all die just as easily in a one-way ticket to somewhere, and anywhere's a better place than where you were.

I understand. Greyhounds may be late, but they never punch or yell.

What To Do About You

What To Do About You

Jessie sat at her keyboard, staring at the monitor and reading the small black words racing across the white screen. She had only met Donald a few months ago, but she had to admit, so far it had been a wild ride and she was both intrigued and enamored. He did seem genuine, although, can anyone ever truly know someone they've only known online?

She'd thought about this a lot lately, mostly at night, when she was feeling alone and vulnerable. Now, as Jessie read his lovely thoughts, she felt the familiar surge of emotion -- and hormones -- as he deftly fashioned each keystroke into a word, a sensual phrase, of yet another perfectly crafted seduction.

She had to smile. Donald had a gift for writing. He was every bit an artist, only his canvas was the human heart, and his medium, the words.

When he finally stopped typing, she sensed he awaited her reply. Gathering up her thoughts and all of the questions that had been nagging at her, she began ...

"Donald, do I know you? I mean, do I *really, really* know who you are? Sometimes I'm sure I do -- at times, I think I even know you better than you know yourself. But there are other times, like at night and I'm feeling alone, when I wonder if I know you at all."

Jessie hesitated a little too long and Donald began filling the screen again. "Sweetie Pie, c'mon, you have to go with the flow. You do *know* me, Babe, you know you do. Someday, we WILL be together, I promise. But just for now, this is what we have. Talk to me, Sunshine. You know you feel it, the love, I mean. I know I feel it. C'mon, you know I love you, Babe."

Jessie took a deep breath, stretched her mind along with her fingers, and began constructing her own words and thoughts to send across the miles.

"Something is happening, Donald, I will agree. Your words have caught me up in something big and, yes, we've made a real connection here in a very short time. But is this love, Donald? I don't know -- how *can* I know? We've never even seen each other in person. Why is that, Donald?"

Jessie paused for a minute to collect her thoughts and immediately, Donald's words appeared on the screen in front of her. "C'mon now, Babe, you know this is love. This is how everyone *should* fall in love.

You and me, we've learned to know and love each other on the *inside* first -- this way, looks don't get in the way. We love each other for who we are, not for how we appear. Am I right? Get a grip, Babe."

Jessie fought back the tears. If only Donald would write the words she needed most to hear:

"I can't wait another minute, Jess. I'm getting on a plane this afternoon. I need you and I want to be with you. I want to look deep in your eyes and see the love I feel for you reflected back at me.

I feel like I'll die if I can't hold you close and breathe you in. I want to fill up my very soul with you. I love you, Jessie, and I can't live another day without you."

Jessie knew she would never see those words, but Donald had paused again, and she tried once more, "Donald, *do* you really know me? I'm sure you'll say you do, but I believe you only *think* you know me because I'm a writer and you've read some of my work -- but those are only little parts of me, just separate thoughts I've sheared off to rhyme or not rhyme. But Donald, that's NOT knowing me or who I really am -- at least I don't think it is.

Don't you see, Donald, we need to be together. We need to spend some time talking about what's important to each of us, maybe make some plans. It's time, now."

Jessie didn't stop typing this time. Her fingers flew. "One thing more, Donald. Your wants and desires scare the hell out of me sometimes. When that happens, all my instincts tell me to run and never look back. Why won't you come and see me? I do love you, but I want to see you and hold you. Don't you feel that, too?

I'll meet you somewhere, ANYwhere! You pick the place. Where do we go from here, Donald? What do I do about you? Please, take a few minutes. Think about what I'm saying."

Jessie stopped typing and sat back in her chair. Quietly and methodically, she began counting the seconds. Maybe this time, Donald would take her seriously, and take some time to think about what she was saying. One one thousand, two one thousand, three one thousand, four one thou ... she watched as

Donald's thoughts began to fill her screen again, slowly at first, then faster, his fingers gathering speed. He was smooth, she would give him that. But Jessie had already realized something very important. Donald had spent little, or no time at all, thinking about what she said ...

Now, reading fast so the tears wouldn't blur the words, she read something much different than what she really needed to see, "Geez oh man, Jess, what the hell? You're being so Goddamn needy -- it's too bad you feel like that. You know how I feel about you, Babe, but you're moving too fast for me. Maybe we oughta rethink this thing ..."

Jessie had read enough. The last words she read before clicking the Power Off button were, " ... and that's what I really need, so I'm sure you understand, Jess. Just remember, Babe, it's your loss ..."

Thoughts of a Call Girl

Thoughts of a Call Girl

Julie Windom checked her makeup in the mirror of the plane's cramped bathroom. She couldn't see her entire reflection, but she didn't need to. She knew she looked good -- hell, she looked fabulous! She worked out in the best gyms all over the country every day. Why wouldn't she look good?

Julie also could easily afford the tailored outfits she chose to show off her perfect figure, as a result of those daily work-outs, too, she thought proudly.

Only moderately full, the 4:57 to Detroit still promised to be worth several thousand over and above Julie's regular take -- like golden icing on the cake, she thought smugly.

It wasn't all that tough, she thought, merely an amusing parlor game, actually. Play it cool and distant -- they eat it up. The more cool and distant she was, the more interested the poor bastards were.

Of course, the pouty lips, smoky eyes, and the $400 come-fuck-me shoes helped, too, she thought with a knowing smile. Yeah, but she had learned through trial and error, it was the cool and distant that actually reeled them in. The more hands off you seem, the more hands on they want to be. They just can't resist.

She makes a mental note to herself: *(Remember to buy a few more shares of Maybelline tomorrow -- hmmm, maybe L'Oreal, as well.)* They both saved my ass more than a few times.

Okay, Julie thought, I'll make Detroit by eight. Ought to be able to do the guy there with no trouble, then cab it back to the hotel, shower and reapply my face. Easy. I'll still have time to take the elevator up to twelve for the john in 12 C. Piece of cake. Then I'll sock another six big ones in the pocket of the suitcase before the 11:30 to Reno. Sweet.

Satisfied with her makeup, Julie replaced the smile with a cool and distant look, closed the bathroom door behind her, and returned to her first class seat beside the wealthy bragging and boring prospect in seat 3A.

A Penny for His Thoughts

A Penny for His Thoughts

Libby sat scowling into her medium extra sugar, extra cream, Mocha Java Swirl Espresso. The small round table wobbled with an audible racket as she shifted the hot paper cup from her left hand to her right, and then back again.

Oh, what I wouldn't give for a folded piece of cardboard to shove under that stupid short table leg for stability -- and some blessed silence! She thought to herself, her attitude nearly as steaming as the coffee was.

Libby had to admit, she had never been any good at reading Richard's silence. She tried to remember how long it had been since she and Richard had talked to each other about anything, other than when the dry cleaning should be picked up, or whether the trash cans had been put out by the curb on Tuesday mornings.

She sighed. Sometimes, what is not said says way more than what IS said.

She almost didn't want to know what was behind the silence. There was a time when she would have just asked, "Hun, what's wrong? Is there something we need to talk about?" But not anymore. The silence had gone on too long now. Besides, there were times when she did politely ask, "What's up, Richard?"

Richard always answered the same, "Nothing, Elizabeth. Nothing at all."

Maybe she should just let well-enough alone. Truth is, she was afraid to ask him the exact words, "What is *wrong*?" now. After all, they weren't married, only living together, and had been for five years. Whatever was *wrong* would probably hurt and not be something she even wanted to hear. Then again, she thought, maybe it's something I *need* to hear.

Libby's imagination was turning somersaults as she tried to imagine how the conversation might go:

First I would smile and ask, "Richard? How about a penny for your thoughts?"

He would most likely say, "Elizabeth? Let's not play games. Would you like to tell me where you're going with this?"

Then, I would say, "Well, you walk around in silence these days, Richard. You never talk to me anymore. Tell me what's going on in your mind ... and in your life, while you're at it."

Richard would probably get very haughty at this point. "Elizabeth, you're being ridiculous. Let's stop all of this foolishness, shall we? What time is dinner?"

Then, naturally, I would try again, "Talk to me, Richard ... you know, a penny for your thoughts.

Would five or six cents get me the truth and maybe spare my feelings just a bit? Richard, come on, play along. How about two nickels then, that's ten cents. Would that sweeten the pot? Or perhaps, three dimes for two or three honest thoughts -- tell me what you're thinking right now, this very minute."

Of course, Richard doesn't like it when I use sarcasm, so he would probably be extremely angry at this point, Libby thought. "Oh for God's sake, Elizabeth, stop it! I don't know what's gotten into you today! That's enough -- you don't want to push me! You may not like what I have to say. Do NOT push me, Elizabeth ..."

If that is truly what he would say, I still wouldn't be able to stop myself, "Okay, Richard, two quarters then. I do want to know. Will that give me your thoughts?

Wait, I'll even up it to a dollar for one clear, *loving* thought, that's all I want ... it's all I need, but it has to be the truth, Richard. I have to know the truth. What is going on in that head of yours? Do you still love me, Richard?"

Libby slammed back to reality when the hot, medium, extra sugar, extra cream, Mocha Java Swirl Espresso suddenly belched all over her hands, the wobbly noisy table, her lap, and the floor. She hadn't even realized she was doing it, but during the brief interlude into her imagination, she had squeezed her paper cup hard out of both rage and pent up frustration.

As Libby helped the waitress mop up the mess on the table, she couldn't help thinking, "I would never tell him this now, but he could have had me and everything I own forever if, just once, he had talked to me, lovingly talked to me, and told me the truth ...

Men and Boys

Men and Boys

The moments are rare, but when the mower is
silent and the hammer and nails have joined the
drill and other tools in the garage, my eyes can get
hell bent on persuading the rest of me that they don't
see a man enjoying his later years, but the child the
man once was.

It's a brief insight, mind you, but when I'm allowed to
see, it's a treasured glimpse into a life that I wasn't
privy to share.

Today, out on the front lawn, I saw a young boy, a
precocious lad of perhaps six. His hair was tousled,
and he was both barefoot and shirtless, tying rags to
the tail of a kite.

Then he was running, racing with the wind, a huge
grin plastered across his face, with delight oozing from
every pore. Then, just as quickly, the vision was gone
and I was left staring in awe at an aging giant, a
grown man at home in his own skin, and merely flying
a kite with a grandson.

I love how those magic moments get flash-frozen and locked away by an efficient mind where they'll suspend like the fruit in a gelatin salad. There, they'll patiently wait until we have a need to revisit them, as we so often do.

I find it astonishing how easily the senses can pick the lock of those moments we've locked away and, once freed, how quickly those same moments are then breathed back to life.

Once they are free, sometimes we cry, sometimes we smile, sometimes we only sigh, but it's okay. Memories seek their validation and we must give them that. Only then can they diminish to a size where we can put them back away and go on with life.

Today, once more I was reminded, there really is no difference between a man and a boy -- only the years between, and the price of their toys.

When It's Over

When It's Over

Sydney Sterling was free at last. She was also stunned, as she soaked up an errant tear into her tissue.   She had just left the courthouse and was walking down the twelve stone steps to the street below to hail a cab.

Sydney had always heard that divorce brought mixed feelings, but she had *never* figured that her feeling of choice would be sadness -- God knows, the marriage had been dying for years.

Still, the sadness did puzzle her. Sydney had always thought when she finally found the nerve to leave Walter, her own main emotion would be one of elation, especially once the judge signed the decree stating that she was finally a free woman.

As she got in the taxi, Sydney gave the driver her new address and shut the door. It's all so strange, she thought. You meet someone, you fall in love, and with all of the best intentions, you believe it will last forever and ever.

Over time, things happen -- you don't even see it coming. You both get busy, tired, and things get all out of focus. Then your world implodes and everything in it pushes and pulls and, with no warning at all, what's left squeezes right between you. And, without ever realizing that it's happening, at some vague point along the way, you both change and suddenly it's over. You're only shadows of who you were, and avoiding each other because of who you've become -- strangers sharing the same house.

You don't really know *how* you know it's over, but you do, she thought. For her, the awareness came slowly. With the certainty and final resignation of a child learning there's no Santa Claus or Easter Bunny, she just knew.

Their breakfast table, once a venue for long dreamy stares and coffee-flavored kisses, had awkwardly become a wordless stage for reading the paper and eating breakfast. She simply realized one morning that the ticking clock on the wall and the crackling of his sports pages were the only sounds left between them at all.

Wiping a fresh tear away with the back of her hand, Sydney recalled the smell of his shirt when she used to bury her face there. She could also remember the touch of his hands on her body, as if they had a life of their own. With a sigh, she realized that both had silently slipped to wherever memories go to gather dust. There they'll stay, fading and finally forgotten among all the broken shards of boredom and used-to-be's.

Sydney sighed. She knew she would miss the nights, and all the love they had made -- at least for awhile, anyway. She remembered all too well their perfect fit, how his body and hers breathed and moved as one.

I don't know really how I knew it was over, she
thought with an uninvited sob. Maybe it was the
nights and the way they used to be that finally gave
the *knowing* life --no, it was all of it together, because
all of it was gone. That's what made me know it was
really over.

Whatever it was, Sydney thought sadly, it broke my
heart just the same . And like the ocean tides on a
favorite beach, love receded with all of the other
yesterdays and Sydney wished she could trade all her
tomorrows to have it back.

Finally, she understood why she was feeling sad -- and
giving her tears their freedom, Sydney grieved for the
death of love.

The Fall of Life

The Fall of Life

Anna McGee was signing a birthday card for her oldest daughter at the kitchen table and enjoying a late morning cup of coffee.

The card was lovely, with pastel rosebuds, delicate greenery, and threaded all around the edges by dainty ecru ribbon. Inside, was one of the most touching verses Anna had ever seen.

She had spent nearly the whole morning in the card store yesterday, laughing at the silly ones, crying over the sad ones, and then she suddenly saw it. She found the one card that captured her sentiments exactly. It was truly the perfect card, all about maternal love, and the pride she felt in the woman and mother Chelsea had become.

Then something odd occurred to her -- Friday, Chelsea would be thirty-eight. The thought caught Anna by surprise, like a sucker-punch, and she couldn't catch her breath for a minute. Oh, it wasn't that Chelsea would be thirty-eight. No, it was more than that. Anna was exactly twenty years older than her daughter, which meant that Anna would be fifty-eight on Friday.

She had never been one who minded getting older, but this year, it felt different. My God, she thought, I'm now in the fall of my life, and I didn't even see it coming. How did I get here so quickly?

Anna laid the pen down on top of the birthday card on the table and stared absently out the kitchen window. Wasn't it just yesterday that I was young and crouched at life's starting gate, waiting for the race to begin? All of my plans, my hopes and dreams were all stretched out before me. Wasn't it just yesterday that we were awaiting the arrival of our first-born, Chelsea?

Anna's thoughts turned melancholy as she reached back into the past, just for a visit ...

As a child, she remembered looking up at her grandparents and feeling such awe. These were her daddy's parents. They had to be very special, because her daddy was.

Back then, she thought her grandparents must be as old as the trees. Their hair was snow white and they always came with bottles of pills, which they lined up in a long row on the kitchen counter top.

Being so old, she thought they were probably very wise, too, so she always listened closely to what either of them shared. Her grampa told her stories about what it was like when he was a boy and there were more horses on the streets than there were cars. He said they didn't have TV's back then. They read books and played games at the kitchen table when it rained.

When it was sunny, they played a lot of outside games, or climbed trees, or went skinny dipping in the pond. She smiled as she remembered the wonderful way grampa explained everything to her, so she could almost see what he was describing, just through his words.

Yes, Anna thought, they were old, but I adored them and I saw them through eyes full of love. I never tired of hearing their stories. I remember going for ice cream cones at the dairy store with them, and hearing grandma hum while she baked pies, and watching grampa puff on his curved pipe that smelled so pungent and good.

Then another sobering thought hit Anna. I am now older than my grandparents were when they passed away. Oh, how I miss them, and suddenly she realized she wanted to be just like them.

Time moves so quickly. No, not in the days of our youth. Then, time only gently nudges us forward towards the finish line and we hardly notice time at all. Then, slowly at first, then faster, life grows until it's full and busy and then things change. Where time used to stop us in our tracks, we suddenly learn just how fast it really does go -- like the thirty-eighth birthday of your oldest child.

Here in the fall of my life, time has simply caught up with me -- it merely caught me off guard, that's all. I have a few regrets, Anna thought. There are things I wish I hadn't done, things I should have done, and things I wish I had done differently. But there are also the many wonderful things that I'm happy to have done, and I'm glad I had the chance to do them.

Anna took another sip of her coffee, which had turned ice cold in her cup. I don't know how long my fall will last, and I certainly have no promises that I will ever see winter, but I do know I've enjoyed my life ... and damn, it's not over yet! From now on, I'm going to treat every day with renewed appreciation.

There are things I still want to accomplish, dreams that can still come true, and children and grandchildren to hug and tell my stories to. Anna smiled. I'm so fortunate to have a wonderful man in my life to share it all with, too.

She remembered what her mother used to say, "Life is a gift, baby girl. How we live it, well, that is our gift to ourselves." Now, many years later, that finally made perfect sense, she thought, as she sent a silent thank you to her mother.

Anna sighed. Okay, that's it -- no more wasted minutes. I'm going to pour myself another cup of coffee, put a stamp on this birthday card and then I'll call Chelsea. After that, I'm going to be busy opening more of my gift ...

About the Author:

A native of Ohio, CJ Heck currently lives in Du Bois Pennsylvania. She is a published poet, writer, blogger, and children's author, who loves writing fiction and nonfiction short stories, memoirs and personal essays. She is also a Vietnam War widow.

For more information about CJ, or to invite her to your school or organization, please visit her website or call 814-249-1777.

Barking Spiders Poetry for Children:
www.barkingspiderspoetry.com

www.ingramcontent.com/pod-product-compliance
Lightning Source LLC
Chambersburg PA
CBHW071401170626
46811CB00003B/1218